SPACE HIJACK!

Nancy Robison
illustrated by
Edward Frascino

Lothrop, Lee & Shepard Co. / New York
A Division of William Morrow & Co., Inc.

To Bob—
who took me to the stars!

Text copyright © 1979 by Nancy Robison

Illustrations copyright © 1979 by Edward Frascino

Library of Congress Cataloging in Publication Data

Robinson, Nancy.
  Space hijack!

  SUMMARY: When a mysterious passenger hijacks their Moon shuttle, Mark and Ted use the difference in gravity to escape from his see-through space people.
  [1. Science fiction]   I. Frascino, Edward.   II. Title.
PZ7.R5697Sp   [E]   78-24218
ISBN 0-688-41897-X
ISBN 0-688-51897-4 lib. bdg.

Printed in the United States of America.

First Edition
1 2 3 4 5 6 7 8 9 10

CONTENTS

1

BLAST OFF

"In a minute we'll be on our way
to the Moon!" Mark said.

"I'm scared," Ted said.

"Relax," said Mark. "I'll tell you
a riddle. If a spaceship carrying red
paint collides with a spaceship
carrying blue paint, what will the crew be?"

"I give up," said Ted.

"Marooned!" Mark said, laughing.
"Blue and red make maroon, and the
crew would be marooned in space."
"Very funny," Ted said. "But I don't
feel like laughing. Are you sure you
have our experiment?"

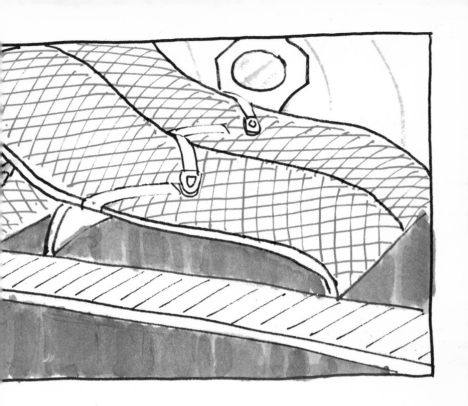

"Here, under my seat," Mark said.
"Winner of the Whole Earth Science
    Fair. Aren't we lucky to win the
    first prize, a trip to the Moon?"
"If we're so lucky," Ted said,
    "why do I feel so scared?"

The man across the aisle looked pale.

Ted leaned over. "It's all right, mister. I know how you feel."

The man scowled.

"Beep!" he said.

Ted nudged Mark.

"What is it?" Mark asked.

"That man beeped at me," Ted said.

Mark laughed. "That reminds me of a joke. Why did the astronaut eat a sandwich?"

Ted shook his head.

"Because it was launchtime!" Mark howled.

Ted wasn't laughing.

"It's launch time now, so what are
the other passengers and the crew
doing out there on the ground?"

Mark looked out the porthole
where Ted was pointing.
"Something's wrong!" he said.
"I knew it!" Ted cringed.
"Stop the launch!"
"It's too late," Mark said.
"We're going to blast off!"

2

THE MYSTERIOUS PASSENGER

The safety belt sign went off.

"Put on your magnetic shoes," Mark said.

"We'll ask Captain Lovejoy what's up."

Ted followed Mark to the cockpit.

They knocked on the door.

A muffled voice said, "Come in."

"Sir," Mark said, "Moonship took off

without the other passengers and

the crew. Is something wrong?"

Ted tapped Mark on the back.

"Wait a minute, Ted," Mark said.

"Give Captain Lovejoy a chance to answer."

"He can't," Ted said. "He's tied up on the floor behind you."

"What?" Mark whirled around.

"Captain, what are you doing there?"
Captain Lovejoy couldn't talk. A
gag was around his mouth.
"We'll untie you," Mark said.
"Beep...No-you-won't." The man in
the captain's seat turned around.
"It's the Beeper!" Ted shouted.

The man pulled off a mask.

His head swiveled around.

"Look!" Mark said. "He has
extra eyes in the back of his head.
He looks like something
from outer space!"

"Beep...I-am-from-outer-space,"
said the man. "And-that-
is-where-we-are-going."

"Oh no," said Ted.

"We've been hijacked!"

3

HIJACKED!

"Hey, we're going away from the Moon!"
Mark said. "How can that be?"
"Beep...I-have-reset-the-course."
"But where are we going?" Ted said.
"Beep...To-my-spaceship."
The spaceman took off his coat.
"Wow!" Mark said. "You can see
right through him!"
The man got out of the chair. Then
he popped up to the ceiling!

"Where's he going?" Ted asked.

"I guess he's lightweight," Mark said.
"Without the coat to hold him down, he
floats."

The spaceman hung from the ceiling
like a chandelier. Now he waved an
object that looked like a laser gun.

"Beep . . . One-of-you-
will-guide-this-ship."

"Not me," Ted said.

"Flying makes me sick."

"Beep . . . You-sit-by-the-lookout port."

Ted sat down and covered his eyes.

"I can't look."

"Beep... You-" the man said to Mark,
"sit-at-the-computer-panel."

Mark sat in front of the panel of
lights and buttons. A red light on
the control panel lit up.

Ted looked out the porthole.

"Hey," Ted shouted, "there are
rocks outside—meteorites!
Oh—they're going to hit us!"

He covered his eyes.

"What'll I do?" Mark asked.

"Beep... Blue-and-yellow-buttons."

"Here goes nothing." Mark pressed
the blue and yellow buttons.

Moonship turned away from the sea
of rocks.

"Whew! That was close," Mark said.

"You can look now," he told Ted.

Slowly Ted took his hands away.

"I just had a terrible idea.

Remember your riddle about the

red and blue space ships colliding?"

Mark nodded. "They got marooned."

"Well, I have a funny feeling

it's about to come true."

MAROONED

"There's a blip on the radar," Mark said.
"We're getting close to something."
"Beep...It-is-my-spaceship."
   Ted looked out. "Do you see it?" he
   whispered.
"Not a thing," Mark answered. Ted said,
"Good—I thought I needed glasses."
"Turn Moonship around," Mark yelled,
"there's nothing out there."

"Fire-retro-rockets-for-docking."

Mark pushed the buttons. They stopped.
Ted looked out. "Hey, there *is* a space
ship out there. It's transparent,
like him. It's not moving."

"Beep...It-has-no-power. You-will-
give-me-your-Atomic-Batteries."

"But the AB's make Moonship go. How
will we get back?"

"Beep... You-don't-matter. I-must-
get-these-Moon-diamonds-to-my-planet."

"Moon diamonds? What for?" Ted asked.

"They-are-the-purest-form-of-carbon.
My-planet-needs-them-for-power."

"Have you been mining our Moon?"

Mark asked.

"Beep... You-ask-too-many-questions.

Get-me-the-batteries."

"Can't we talk this over?" Ted said.

The spaceman dangled from the ceiling.

He pointed his gun at Captain Lovejoy.

"I guess he means it," Mark said.

The boys took out the batteries.

"Now what?" Ted asked.

"Beep...Give-them-to-me."

The boys handed them over. With the weight to hold him down, the spaceman could walk on the floor. He stepped into the air lock and vanished.

5

A DESPERATE PLAN

"What do we do now?" Ted said.

"Untie Captain Lovejoy. He'll know
what to do."

They untied the captain. He sat
up and rubbed his head.

"Have we landed on the Moon?" he asked.

"No, we've been hijacked," Mark said.

"And now we're marooned," Ted said.

"The spaceman stole our AB's."

"He can't do that!" the captain said.

He tried to stand up.

"What hit me? I'd better lie down."

"You rest, sir. We'll be right back
with the batteries." Mark pulled Ted
into the air lock.

"Why did you say that?" Ted said. "The
Beeper won't give you back the AB's."

"Then we'll just have to take them!"
Mark said. "Follow me."

Mark and Ted crossed into the
see-through space ship. Instantly they
popped up to the ceiling.

"Help! What's happening?" Ted said.

"Magnetic shoes won't work on plastic
floors," Mark said. "We're floating here
the way the spaceman did in Moonship."

"Don't look down," Ted said. "It's a see-through floor and a straight drop to nothing." He closed his eyes.

"Open your eyes," Mark said.

"No," Ted said. "It makes me dizzy."

"I think you'd better," Mark said. "We're surrounded."

Staring up at the boys were six see-through people. They all had four eyes.

"Oh-oh," said Ted.

"You can't pull a fast one on them," Mark said. "They can see everything."

"I don't like this place," Ted said. "I feel like a fly."

6

THE CHASE

"There are the Moon diamonds!"
Mark said. "Let's take them."
"That's stealing," Ted said.
"Those people stole them from our
Moon. The diamonds belong to us.
And with the heavy diamonds in our
pockets, we won't float any more."
"Good idea," Ted agreed. They pulled
themselves over to the diamonds and
filled their pockets.

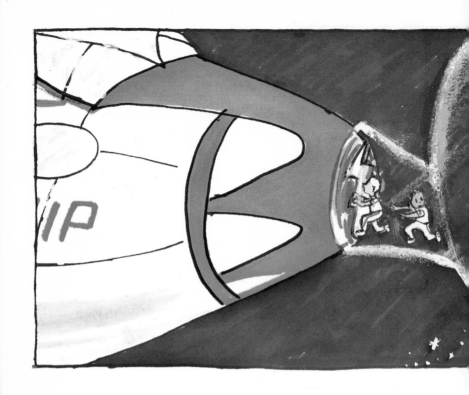

They came down from the ceiling.

The space people came toward them.

"Don't look now," Ted said, "but

I think they're after us."

"Run for it," Mark said.

"Where?"

"Back to Moonship."

They ran back to their own ship.

The space people chased them.

As soon as they entered Moonship

the space people popped up

to the ceiling.

"That takes care of them," Mark said.

"Now let's get those batteries!"

The boys ran back to the spaceship. They
went to the control room. The man was
working the control panel.

"What do we do now?" Ted whispered.

"There's his gun on the table," Mark
said. "We'll grab it and make him
give us the batteries."

Quietly they worked their way over
to the table. Mark got the gun and
said, "Hands up!"
The roar of rockets drowned his voice.
"Mark!" Ted shouted. "This spaceship
  just took off!"
"Then we'll have to hijack it!"

7

A CHANGE OF PLANS

Mark poked the spaceman with the gun.
"As the rug said to the floor,
stick 'em up, I've got you covered!"
The spaceman turned around.
"What-are-you-doing-here? Beep...
Put-that-water-pistol-down."
"Water pistol?" Mark said. "I
thought it was a laser gun."
"Beep...I-didn't-want-to-hurt-
anyone," said the spaceman.

"Take us to Earth!" Ted said.

"Beep...Earth-is-dangerous. Someday-
you-will-slip-off-that-round-globe-
and-fall-into-space."

"No we won't. We have gravity to
hold us on," Ted told him.

"Beep...On-my-planet-we-live-inside.
No-danger-of-falling-off."

"We want to go to Earth," Mark said.

"You-should-have-stayed-on-your-
ship. Now-you-will-go-to-our-planet."
Ted moaned. "I'm going to walk around
on ceilings for the rest of my life!"
The spaceman was searching the ship
with his four eyes. He looked angry.

"Beep...Where are my people?"

"We know but we won't tell you,"
Ted said bravely.

"Beep-beep-beep-beep!" The spaceman
shouted. He shook Ted's arms, hard.
The diamonds fell out of Ted's pocket.
Ted floated to the ceiling.
Suddenly he laughed.

"Now you can't reach me,
and I still won't tell."
Mark looked up at him. "But Ted,
we have to tell. We can't leave
Captain Lovejoy marooned in space!"
Ted sighed. "You're right. Tell him
we'll make a trade, his people for us."

8
THE TRADE

They pulled up next to Moonship. The
man said, "Beep...Get-my-people."
"You can have them if you can catch
them," Mark said. He crossed into
Moonship. Ted floated over.
The little people were still stuck to
the ceiling like balloons.
Ted came down. "At least I can walk
on the floor again!"
"I'll reverse the air pressure," Mark said.

He turned a switch. The people
dropped off the ceiling. They blew
out the door like puffed wheat.
"They're floating in space! And the
spaceship has gone after them."

"Now we can go too," Mark said.

"How? He has our AB's," Ted said.

"We have more. Don't you remember?"

"We do? Where?" Ted asked.

"In our science experiment."

"But then our experiment

   won't work," Ted argued.

"If we don't use them, *we* won't work!"

   Ted yanked out all their batteries.

   Mark put them into the control panel.

The boys woke Captain Lovejoy.

"How are you feeling, sir?" Ted asked.

"Much better." The captain smiled.

"Now let me fly this ship back to
good old Earth."

Ted strapped himself into his webcouch. "We came all this way for nothing."

Mark emptied his pockets. "I wouldn't call a pocketful of diamonds nothing."

"Hey, that's right!" Ted laughed. "And we learned two scientific facts."

"What?" asked Mark.

"There *is* a man in the Moon," Ted began, and Mark chimed in,

"and there *are* diamonds in the sky!"

About the Author

NANCY ROBISON has always been fascinated with outer space. *Space Hijack!* is her second book for Lothrop. Her first, with the same illustrator, was *UFO Kidnap!* Mrs. Robison is married and the mother of four athletic sons. She lives in San Marino, California.

About the Illustrator

EDWARD FRASCINO is a New Yorker whose cartoons regularly liven the pages of *The New Yorker* magazine. He has illustrated many children's books, including Nancy Robison's *UFO Kidnap!* He is also the illustrator of E. B. White's *The Trumpet of the Swan*, and the author of one children's book, *Eddie Spaghetti*.